COOPER

flying dog

montse ganges
emilio urberuaga

Published in 2009 by Windmill Books, LLC
303 Park Avenue South, Suite # 1280, New York, NY 10010-3657

Copyright © Combel Editorial, S.A.
Copyright © Montse Ganges (text)
Copyright © Emilio Urberuaga (illustrations)
Credits: Written by Montse Ganges
           Illustrated by Emilio Urberuaga

                        Publisher Cataloging Data
Ganges, Montse
        Cooper, flying dog / M. Ganges and E. Urberuaga.
               p. cm. – (Cooper)
        Summary: Cooper the dog's wagging tail propels him up to the highest shelf,
where the dog biscuits are kept.
        ISBN 978-1-60754-239-1 – ISBN 978-1-60754-240-7 (pbk.)
ISBN 978-1-60754-241-4 (6-pack)
        1. Dogs—Juvenile fiction   [1. Dogs—Fiction]   I. Urberuaga, Emilio   II. Title   III. Series
        [E]—dc22

Printed in the United States of America

For more great fiction and nonfiction, go to www.windmillbooks.com.

alphabet
soup

an imprint of

WINDMILL
BOOKS
New York

Cooper's house has a balcony
with a view of the sea,
which glimmers in the sunshine.
But Cooper prefers a spot in the
kitchen with a view of the Biscuit Jar.

Every afternoon, Cooper sits
staring at the Biscuit Jar,
which is kept on the Highest Shelf.
When he thinks about the taste of the
biscuits, Cooper wags his tail so fast
that his whole body shakes.

4

Today the neighbor's parrot has come over to keep him company. "Are those biscuits really *that* good?" he asks.

"These are the best biscuits in the world,"
Cooper declares,
in complete seriousness.
And again he wags his tail very fast,
faster than ever . . .
until he takes off with
his bottom in the air.

"I'm getting near the Highest Shelf!"
Cooper cries.
"I'm right behind you!
We're the Biscuit Gang!"
the neighbor's parrot calls enthusiastically.

Cooper and the parrot see themselves
reflected in the glass of the jar.
"Go, Biscuit Gang!"
Cooper exclaims.
And the parrot flaps his wings and cries,
"Open it! Quick!"

But a dog cannot unscrew the
lid of a jar, and neither can a parrot.
What now? The Biscuit Gang
doesn't know how to open jars.
"What about pushing the
jar onto the floor?"
the parrot suggests.

But then a ray of sun hits the
glass and it shines brilliantly.
The light bounces back and
illuminates Cooper and the parrot.
Their eyes light up.
They forget about the Biscuit Jar.

Cooper grabs his friend and
they follow the sparkling light.
They fly out the window and
the fresh air feels wonderful.
"Look, I can fly anywhere I want!"
Cooper discovers.

Wagging his tail,
he heads for the beach.
He soars up to the clouds and
swoops down close to the waves.
He is happy.

The neighbor's parrot doesn't like waves.
He's afraid of being splashed
or pulled under the water.
He stays on the beach, sunbathing.

22

Cooper flies along and calls hello to the
fish that stick their heads out of the water.
"This is amazing! A flying dog!"
they exclaim.
If they had one, the fish would give
Cooper a Supersized Biscuit.